Rapunzel and the Billy Goats

For Henry, Max and Edward

First published in 2013
by Wayland

Text copyright © Hilary Robinson 2013
Illustration copyright © Simona Sanfilippo 2013

Wayland
338 Euston Road
London NW1 3BH

Wayland Australia
Level 17/207 Kent Street
Sydney, NSW 2000

The rights of Hilary Robinson to be identified as the Author
and Simona Sanfilippo to be identified as the Illustrator of this Work have
been asserted by them in accordance with the Copyright, Designs and
Patents Act, 1988.

Series Editor: Louise John
Cover design: Emil Dacanay
Design: Lisa Peacock
Consultant: Shirley Bickler

A CIP catalogue record for this book is available from the British Library.

ISBN 9780750268653

Printed in China

Wayland is a division of Hachette Children's Books,
an Hachette UK Company

www.hachette.co.uk

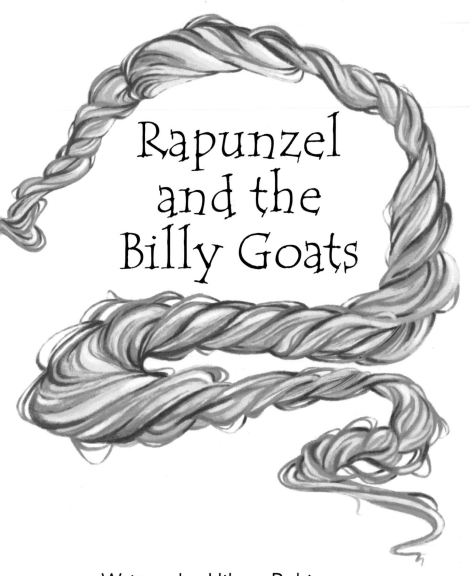

Rapunzel
and the
Billy Goats

Written by Hilary Robinson
Illustrated by Simona Sanfilippo

WAYLAND

Three billy goats were grazing,
when they stopped and looked around.
They could hear a lady singing
and said, "What a lovely sound!"

They set off to a wooden bridge
by a meadow of green grass.

"Stop right there!" a mean troll yelled.
"I will not let you pass!"

He'd built a tower by the bridge
with no door or winding stair.

And hidden at the top of it,
was Rapunzel with long hair.

The goats all watched the troll
as he called up to the maid,
"Rapunzel! Let down your hair!"
Then he scrambled up the braid.

One day a handsome prince rode by,
and stopped to pick a flower.

He heard Rapunzel's lovely song,
and rode up to the tower.

Rapunzel whispered down to him,
"Please help me out of here!"
She told him what the troll had done
and how she lived in fear.

The prince said kindly, "I'll be back
with a rope to set you free!"

But the troll woke up and shouted,
"You will not escape from me!"

The troll climbed up the braid
and he cut Rapunzel's hair!

He left her in the wood and said,
"The prince won't find you there!"

The goats took care of her and they
would rest beside the spring.
She, in turn, made friends with them,
and taught them how to sing!

The prince came back and shouted up,
"Rapunzel! Where are you?"

The troll let down Rapunzel's hair –
and trapped the Prince there, too.

The troll was cross and threw the prince
into brambles where he lay,
blinded by thorns, until he woke
the next bright sunny day.

He could hear the goats all singing
and Rapunzel's voice as well.

He stumbled through the leaves and trees,
and found them in the dell.

Rapunzel held him in her arms,
as he lay beside a tree.

Her tears of joy dripped in his eyes
and he found that he could see!

They fell in love! As for the troll: well, he was last seen heading for far-off shores, while our three goats were bridesmaids at the wedding!

START READING is a series of highly enjoyable books for beginner readers. The books have been carefully graded to match the Book Bands widely used in schools. This enables readers to be sure they choose books that match their own reading ability.

Look out for the Band colour on the book in our Start Reading logo.

The Bands are:

Pink Band 1A & 1B

Red Band 2

Yellow Band 3

Blue Band 4

Green Band 5

Orange Band 6

Turquoise Band 7

Purple Band 8

Gold Band 9

START READING books can be read independently or shared with an adult. They promote the enjoyment of reading through satisfying stories, plays and non-fiction narratives, which are supporte.d by fun illustrations and photographs.

Hilary Robinson loves jumbling up stories and seeing how they turn out. Her life is a jumbled up lot of fun, too! Hilary writes books for children and produces radio programmes for BBC Radio 2 and, because she really likes doing both, she really feels as if she is living happily ever after!

Simona Sanfilippo loves to draw and paint all kinds of animals and people. She enjoyed reading illustrated fairytales as a child and hopes you will enjoy reading these fairytale jumbles, too!